Flash

Just Right Reader

Stan and pals swing. But Stan's not like his sloth pals.

He's slick! He's quick! He's fast!

It's fun to fling over the grass.

Let's go!

His pals say, "Stan, you're great!"

When his pals call, he's Flash!

"I'm both! Stan and Flash!"

Yes, let's go dash.

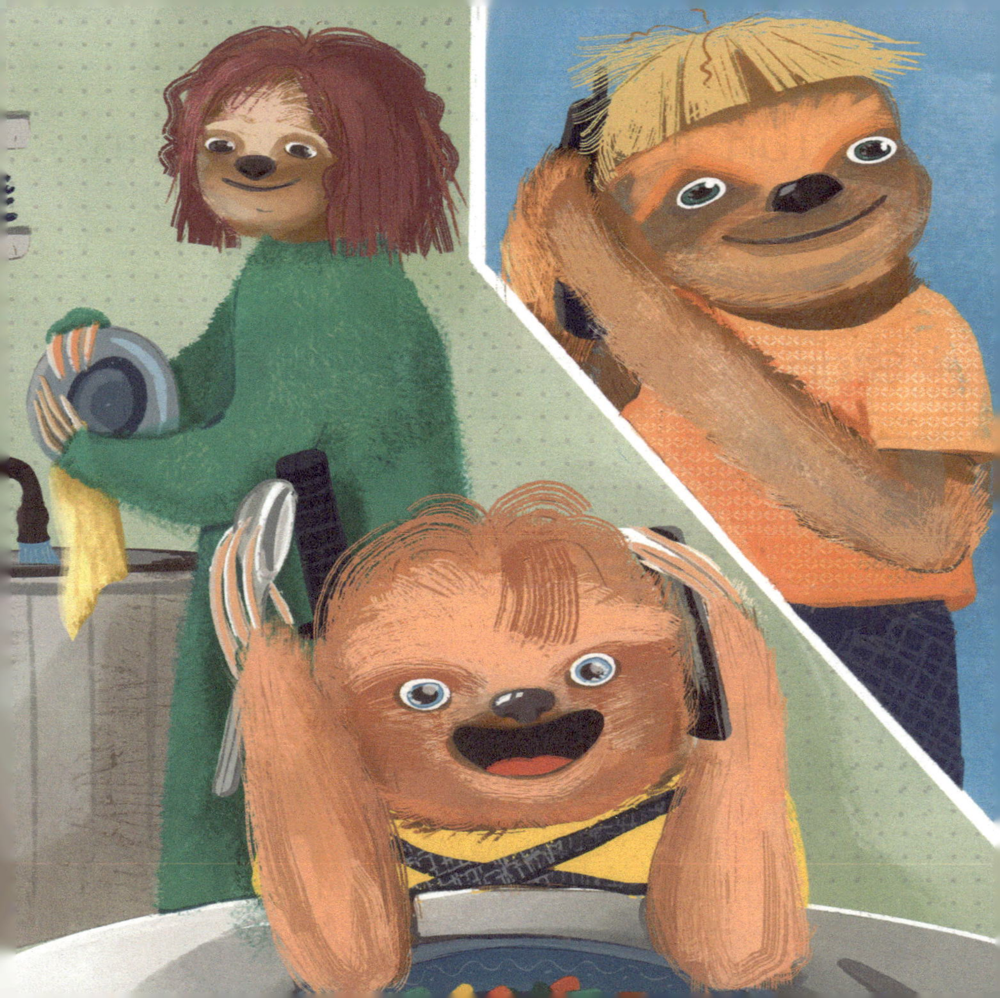

It's fun to bend up and down.
It's fun to run drills.

Stan can't be still. He's got to be fast.

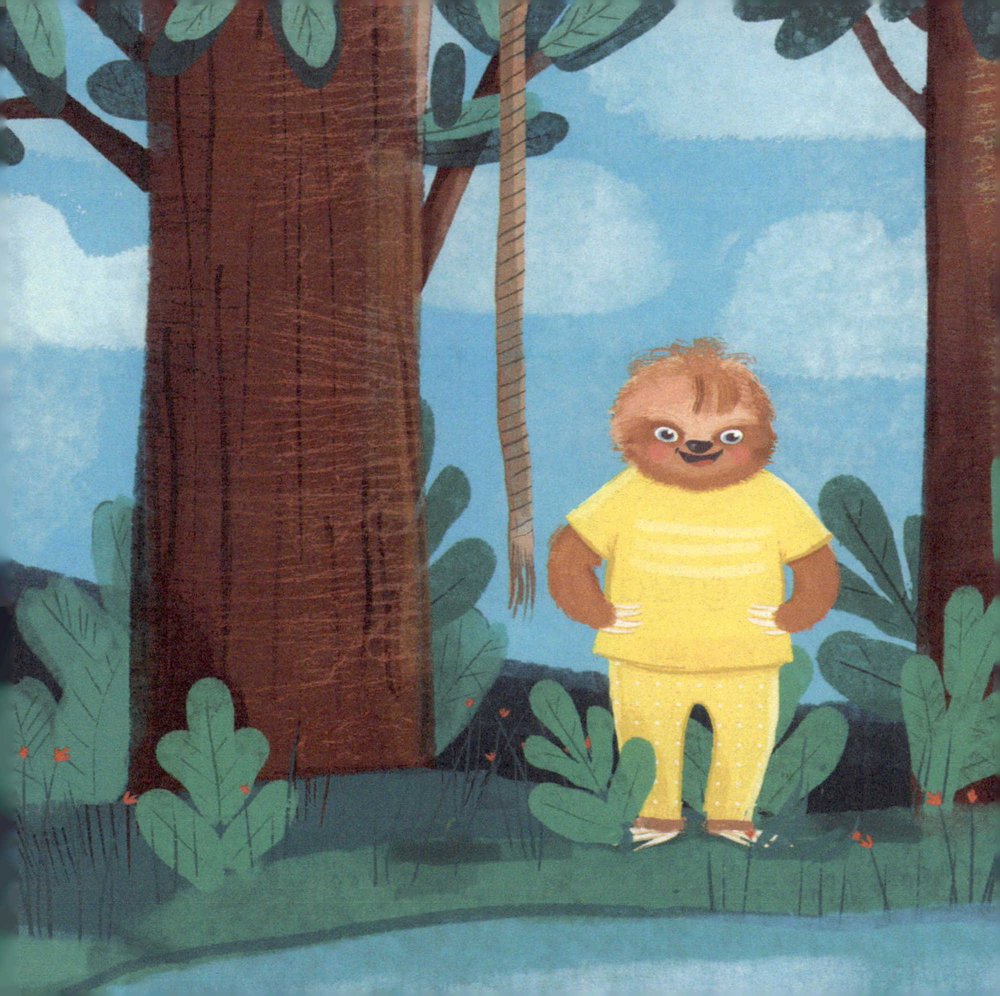

He swings! He can't slip. He can't fall.

It's a trick to go fast. He's the Flash!

"You're great," his pals say.

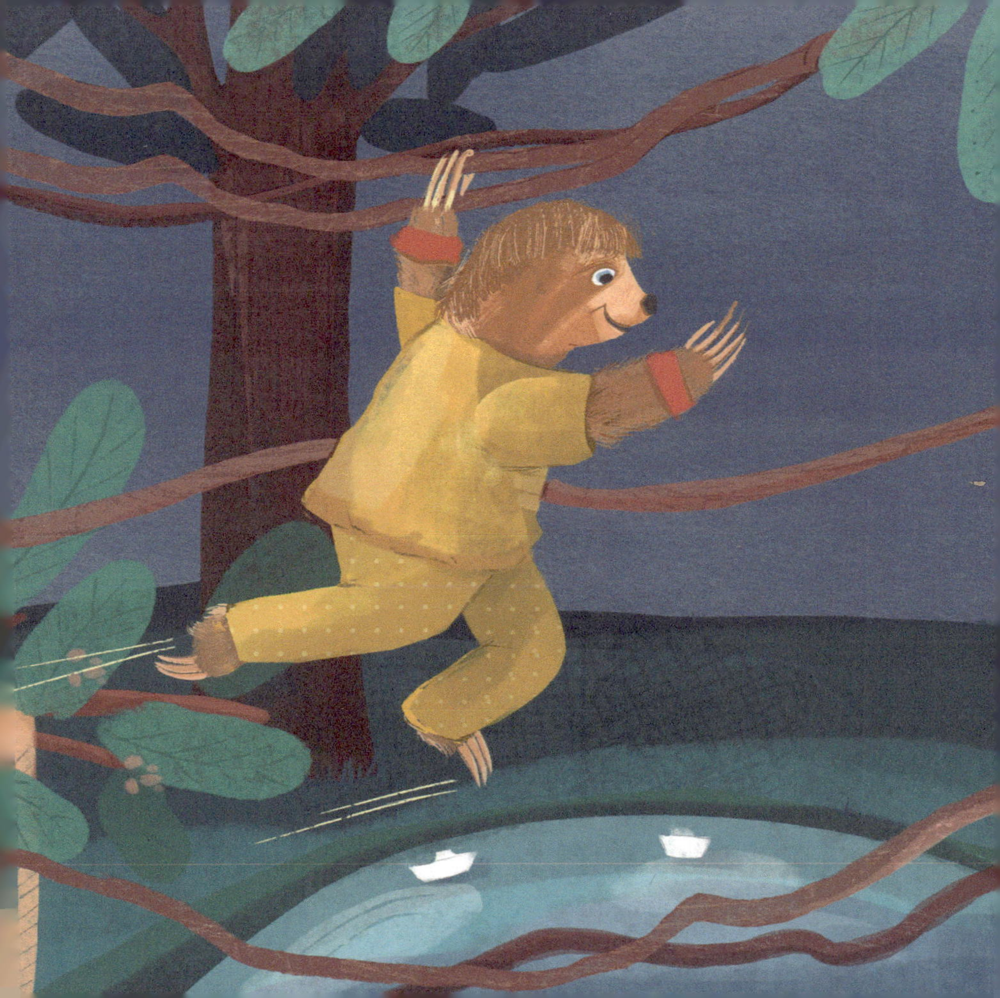

He holds on. He can't fall.

Will he stop? He hasn't yet.

He's the Flash!

His pals yell, "You're great!"

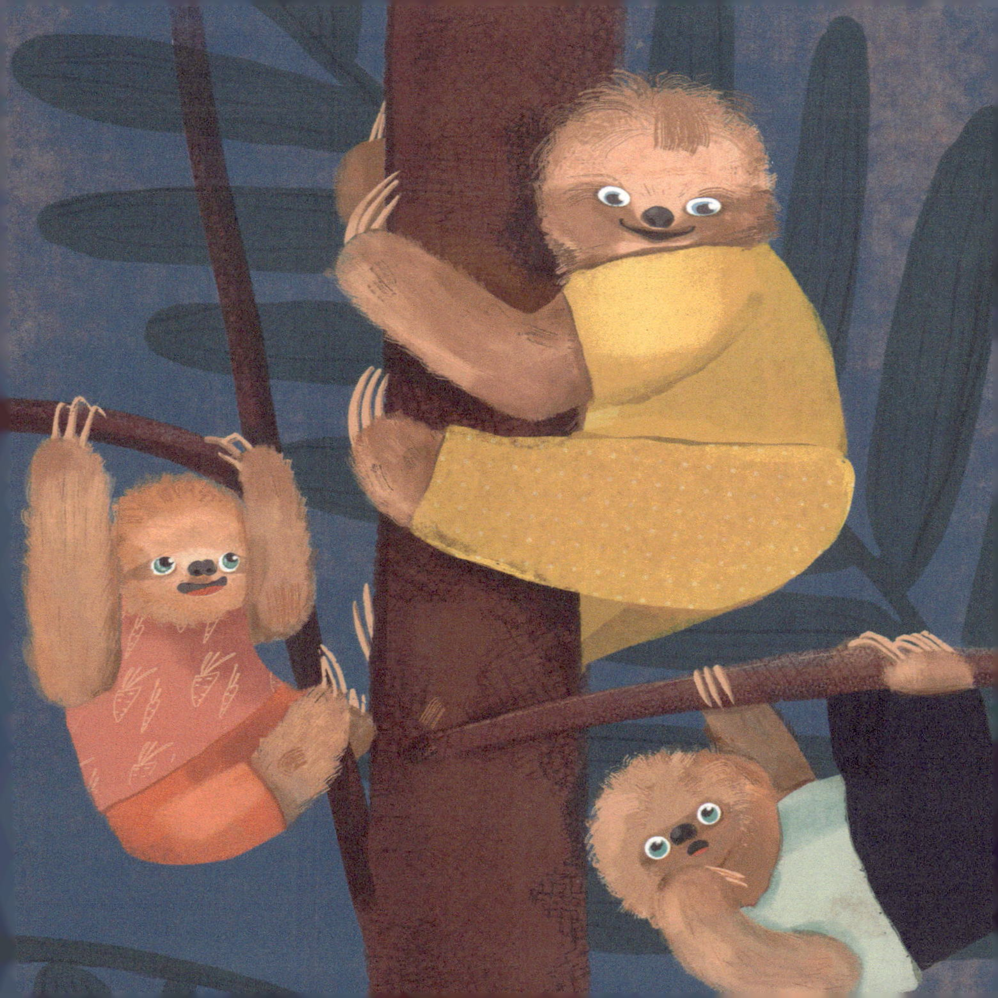

Stan loves to zip. He straps his pals in.

"You're snug? You've a strong grip?" says Stan.

"Let's go!" says Kris.

It's fun! It's great!

Stan and pals zip.

"It's fun," say his pals.

His pals don't fall.

"You're the Flash. You're great!"

Phonics Fun

- Say a word from the word list in the book.
- Write 2 words that make the contraction (e.g., it's, it is).

Comprehension

Did this book make you think of another book? Which one and why?

Decodable Words

can't	it's
don't	let's
hasn't	Stan's
he's	you're
I'm	you've

High Frequency Words

great   love   you're